When I Teach My Monkey How to Dance

Celeste Farris Wissman

Illustrations by Floyd Yamyamin

AuthorHouse™
1663 Liberty Drive
Bloomington, IN 47403
www.authorhouse.com
Phone: 1-800-839-8640

Published by AuthorHouse 09/18/2012

ISBN: 978-1-4772-6035-7 (sc)
       978-1-4772-6038-8 (e)

Library of Congress Control Number: 2012914745

authorHOUSE®

Celeste Farris Wissman is excited to be writing her first children's book about dance. Celeste is the owner and director of Dance With Celeste, her dance studio that she opened in 1999 after receiving her Bachelor of Fine Arts in Dance from Temple University. She also received a Master's Degree in Elementary Education from Holy Family University. Celeste loves her students at Dance With Celeste. Her students were the inspiration in writing this book.

When I teach my monkey how to dance . . .

She always listens to my rule because she likes to go to the dance school.

3

She sometimes dresses very funny, but I don't mind because she's as sweet as honey!

She points her toes very
strong . . .

She never wants to do anything
wrong!

She doesn't have lots of hair to
fit in a bun,
but it doesn't matter because
she's having fun!

7

Working hard on her dance steps day after day, she hardly takes any time to play.

She eats her banana, a healthy snack.

She always has one in her backpack.

She scratches her arm, her
head, and her belly, she is
an animal so sometimes she's
smelly!

Some days during class we don't get very far,

Because like every other monkey she likes to swing on the barre!

She might not look like a graceful dancer,

But to me she is the perfect answer!

The other students might laugh at her but they don't see, just how special my monkey is to me.

When my monkey dances she makes me smile! My smile gets so big, as big as a mile!

When I teach my monkey how to dance I am proud to say, she is my student, I wouldn't have it any other way!!!

CPSIA information can be obtained
at www.ICGtesting.com
Printed in the USA
LVIW010810201012

303580LV00002B